Pebble®

Families
Uncles

by Lola M. Schaefer

Consulting Editor: Gail Saunders-Smith, PhD

Capstone
press®
Mankato, Minnesota

Pebble Books are published by Capstone Press,
151 Good Counsel Drive, P.O. Box 669, Mankato, Minnesota 56002.
www.capstonepress.com

1 2 3 4 5 6 13 12 11 10 09 08

Library of Congress Cataloging-in-Publication Data
Schaefer, Lola M., 1950–
    Uncles / by Lola M. Schaefer. — Rev. and updated.
    p. cm. — (Pebble books. Families)
    Includes bibliographical references and index.
    Summary: "Simple text and photographs present uncles and how they interact
with their families" — Provided by publisher.
    ISBN-13: 978-1-4296-1229-6 (hardcover)
    ISBN-10: 1-4296-1229-0 (hardcover)
    ISBN-13: 978-1-4296-1758-1 (softcover)
    ISBN-10: 1-4296-1758-6 (softcover)
    1. Uncles — Juvenile literature. I. Title. II. Series.
HQ759.94.S35 2008
306.87 — dc22   2007027103

Note to Parents and Teachers

The Families set supports national social studies standards related
to identifying family members and their roles in the family. This
book describes and illustrates uncles. The images support early
readers in understanding the text. The repetition of words and
phrases helps early readers learn new words. This book also
introduces early readers to subject-specific vocabulary words, which
are defined in the glossary section. Early readers may need some
assistance to read some words and to use the Table of Contents,
Glossary, Read More, Internet Sites, and Index sections of the book.

Table of Contents

Uncles

Uncles are brothers
of mothers and fathers.

Uncles live nearby
or far away.

8

Nieces and Nephews

Uncles have nieces
and nephews.

What Uncles Do

Uncle Kyle plays the guitar.

Uncle Tony plays basketball.

Uncle Ted puts together
a puzzle.

Uncle Marc cooks
for a picnic.

Uncle Jeff laughs.

Uncles love.

Glossary

brother — a boy or a man who has the same parents as another child

father — a male parent; an uncle is your father's brother.

mother — a female parent; an uncle is your mother's brother.

nephew — the son of an uncle's brother or sister

niece — the daughter of an uncle's brother or sister

Read More

Easterling, Lisa. *Families.* Our Global Community. Chicago: Heinemann, 2007.

West, Colin. *Uncle Pat and Auntie Pat.* Read-it! Chapter Books. Minneapolis: Picture Window Books, 2006.

Internet Sites

FactHound offers a safe, fun way to find Internet sites related to this book. All of the sites on FactHound have been researched by our staff.

Here's how:

1. Visit *www.facthound.com*
2. Choose your grade level.
3. Type in this book ID **1429612290** for age-appropriate sites. You may also browse subjects by clicking on letters, or by clicking on pictures and words.
4. Click on the **Fetch It** button.

FactHound will fetch the best sites for you!

Index

brothers, 5
cooking, 17
fathers, 5
laughing, 19
loving, 21
mothers, 5
nephews, 9

nieces, 9
playing, 11, 13, 15
Uncle Jeff, 19
Uncle Kyle, 11
Uncle Marc, 17
Uncle Ted, 15
Uncle Tony, 13

Word Count: 44
Grade 1
Early-Intervention Level: 10

Editorial Credits
Sarah L. Schuette, revised edition editor; Kim Brown, revised edition designer

Photo Credits
Capstone Press/Karon Dubke, all